THE TEMPLE OF REMEMBRANCE

THE TEMPLE OF REMEMBRANCE

DIANE SWAFFIELD

The Elonias Foundation

Chapter 1

The Temple of Remembrance

It was a dark night, and as my footsteps echoed upon the stone steps, I hurried into the doorway of the Inner Sanctuary. They had already started, so I made my way silently towards the back and sat down upon the cold stone floor. He was speaking, the one they called the Father of All, dressed in his gown of indigo, and the radiance that emanated from him was so beautiful, as it always was.

I looked momentarily around me, to look lovingly at the Temple that had brought me so much joy, so much sorrow, so much pain, and yet here I was seated in the presence of He that I now knew to be the 'Father of All'. Within me, I held me the knowing of my real true self.

The room was fairly wide, with a long narrow opening to allow the night sky to be visible upon the upper reaches of the room. The night was dark, the moon not yet visible, yet the room seemed somehow so very light with the presence of the wondrous beings that knew us so well.

He speaks of belonging, not to an individual, not to a belief, not to any one thing, but to belong totally within 'all'. He says that belonging can be looked upon as a dependency of thought that allows another to take advantage, but in the belonging to all, there is a knowing that there can never be a separateness of thought, ever.

As He speaks, I attempt to turn inwardly to the belonging of all, but instead I allow a single thought to remind me of my insecurity of letting go of the outward belonging. A simple thought, but yet as it is uttered from my mind, I open my eyes to see Him looking at me, and I know that He knows that I am not yet ready to enter into the oneness of all.

My Inner Being screams to be allowed to be given an opportunity to try again, and yet I can feel the failure welling up within me, which is my fear of letting go of who I believe myself to be. So with a heavy heart, I stand and leave the sanctity of the Inner Chamber.

The untold years of time within the Temple has given to me a peace that I cannot even begin to describe. Failure has no part to play in the uncovering of the Greater Plan, and yet as I look back upon that day of knowing that my inner search has not passed the test of letting go completely, I shall re-enter the Temple of Remembrance once again, and I shall know.

Chapter 2

My mind wanders back to a yesterday in time, and I allow it to flow into the memory of what it needs so desperately to recall. As the memory starts to emerge, I wonder if it will fully release the power of yesterday into now. I wait expectantly, and then I remember...

My mother had always, even before I was born, known that I would be given up to the Temple. As history suggests, the first born son was usually offered to the Temple for service. Only the strong in mind and body was placed before the High Priest for his consideration, and only a small number took the undertaking of initiation into the higher service of the Priesthood.

It was not a natural inclination to let go of my strong bond for my family, and my even stronger bond to my self will. My tenth year brought the severing of all that I held near and dear to me, and my reluctance towards the opportunity to go before the High Priest was obvious, but dismissed by my Mother and Father as being a temporary display of fear.

What was fear? I asked myself. Was it letting go of love, comfort, freedom of thought and action, and all that was familiar and safe? If that is fear, then that is what I felt.

The sun rose that day on a young boy being prepared to be presented, along with many others, to the one they say can see into your very being, with no words being spoken or exchanged.

I was that young boy. I allowed a single thought to emerge from my mind. The thought that I may somehow be rejected from entering the Temple.

This thought began to gain momentum in my mind. If I was rejected, then I could go free, and it was this very thought that brought a sudden sense of excitement at the prospect of being allowed to stay with my family and all whom I knew and loved.

From the mindset of a young boy, I decided there and then, no matter what shame I brought upon myself and my family, I would allow myself to be full of aggression and fear. Yes, that is what I will do, and in doing so, He surely would pass me by.

My hopes were raised at this exciting prospect, and as I stood with my parents at the entrance of the Temple, their tears of joy and emotion had no effect on my need to show a challenging and aggressive response to all within the Temple. With this thought in mind, I felt sure I would soon be home again, where I belonged.

The time was drawing close to leave my family and say my goodbyes. As they put their arms around me, I held onto them so tightly, for I never wanted them to let go, not ever.

I put on a brave front as I stepped away from their loving gaze. It was time to take the first steps into the Temple and be presented to the one who made the decision as to who may or may not enter the Temple of Remembrance for the duration of their life. I took a deep breath...

The doorway to the Temple loomed up before me as a reminder to all that was unknown. The fear that I had felt earlier had returned with a vengeance, and no matter how hard I tried, the fear brought an uncertainty as to how I was to proceed with my plan of rebelliousness. In that moment how I longed to turn back and feel my Mother's arms embracing me, whispering words of love to drive my fear away. The loneliness engulfed me, but I knew I could not turn back.

As I entered through the doorway, I attempted to adjust my eyes to the dim light. There was an eerie silence that quickly gave way to the sound of footsteps. A young woman approached, and gestured for me to follow.

Together we walked through passageway after passageway, seemingly down into the earth itself. After a while, we stopped at a door that led into a small room. The room was sparsely furnished, with just a wooden seat, a pitcher of water and a small vessel.

She asked me to disrobe, and dismissed my youthful modesty with a smile. She waited whilst I took off my garment, and then took the pitcher of water and gently cleansed my body. Then anointed me with the herbal oils contained within the vessel.As she clothed me with a simple white garment which lay upon the wooden seat, she smiled at me as she viewed the finished result. However, through her smile I sensed a sadness that I could not understand.

It was time she said, to go before Him. I followed her once more, feeling my heart pounding in my chest, and also feeling for the first time a sense of pride in myself. Even though I would not be staying, the attention I had received gave me a feeling of being special. This would be a story to remember.

She stopped at a large door which seemed to open, even without her indicating that we were there. I thought this somewhat strange. She told me to go in, but she was unable to follow. So, with bated breath I entered, and it was then that I first saw Him.

It was in this moment that I knew that I had never really lived before, truly lived. His eyes went into the depth of my very being, and love as I had known it was just a shadow to the depth of love that I was now experiencing. I never wanted to leave this place, not ever.

My eyes met His, and His all encompassing love engulfed me. My earlier need for rebelliousness disappeared, as if it had never had a place in my thoughts. Momentarily I lost my identity as I seemed to mould into His very being.

My youthful fears of leaving behind my loving family and all that was known to me was, in an instant, of no consequence. All that I knew was that I never wanted to leave Him. He who knew me so well.

What happened next is hard to recall, except to say that the room and all within it was suddenly transformed and I was no longer in a body of a child, but instead occupied a body of a man.

A sureness rose up within me, and I became aware of the silence of the 'all knowing'. It was then that I knew that time was an illusion.

I had always known Him, and the lifetime to which the child belonged had been viewed through the illusion of time, which brought fear and uncertainty, but my recognition had brought back to me the reality of all.

This moment of 'all knowing' was suddenly snatched from my grasp, and as I struggled to find it again, I realised that I was once again in my body of youth, and He was looking at me, and I knew that He recognised my struggle.

My knees buckled under me as the fear returned of having to leave the immensity of His love. My voice found its sound and uttered the words, "Help me to know again". He smiled and gestured for me to be seated upon the floor.

Time seemed to stand still as His voice spoke softly of the journey ahead. He told me I had to forget the love that I felt for my family and friends that would stop me from really loving. For he said that comparison of love would always enter into my being, and that there could be no comparison, for love was all the same.

From the inner love to the outer, love had to be understood totally. Whilst I still had the memory of love in my heart for another, I would always find a comparison of love and call it total love. Only when I could let go of what I called love, could I find what love really meant.

To release the self from all that was known was the only way to find the totality of self. He asked me if I believed I was strong enough to take on the training of releasing all that was known to me.

As I whispered the word "Yes" I did not even begin to understand the intensity of the struggle that lay ahead, and I wonder, as I reflect on that day, if I had known, would I have left the Chamber and walked away from the most difficult journey I have ever taken? I doubt it.

My body felt cold as the morning light entered in. It took me a moment to gather my senses, but recognition of my surroundings swiftly came back to me. The room stirred to the sounds of five other boys who had also been accepted into the Temple of Remembrance.

I shivered with anticipation of what was to come on this day. Would He come and be with us to instruct us on the ways and means of Inner Wisdom? I convinced myself that He certainly would, for surely He would be our teacher, for were we not the 'chosen ones?' With this thought in mind, I reached out for my robe that I had laid so carefully and proudly by my woven mat. As I placed it upon me, I felt the cold morning give way to its warmth.

My mind went back to the evening before when I was joined by the other boys, and we shared our excitement of what was to come after meeting the Great One. However, our joyous laughter was suddenly interrupted by the rebuke of one of the Holy Ones, who sternly told us that talking indiscriminately was not part of our future life here.

As I looked around me, I saw their faces in the early morning light also showing the anticipation and eagerness that I felt within my own being. I suddenly realised that we were all sharing the same feelings, without any words being spoken. This was so new to me and yet felt so secure.

A sound rang out. A sound so unfamiliar and yet it touched within me an urgency to respond. The door flung open and one of the Holy Ones gestured for us to follow him.

As we moved quietly out into the passageway, I felt the stirring of fear again moving through me, and no matter how I battled to overcome it, the fear became my master. My body responded and my legs seemed to lose their need to move. I willed my mind to return back to the memory of the total love that He emanated, and with this thought the fear slowly began to disappear, and I quietly followed the others to begin Day 1 of my new life.

The Holy One stopped at a door and told us that we were to begin our training of overcoming our pride, our fear and our dignity. He beckoned for me to follow him into the room and told the others to wait. I found myself in a very dark room which appeared empty except for a mat, which lay upon the stone floor. He asked me to remove my garment and to be seated upon the mat.

As I disrobed, I shivered with the cold, and my modesty once again was challenged. He told me that I was to be left within this room without clothing, without food and without water. All that I would have would be my memories of my need to make my body comfortable.

The test was to recognise the power of the needs of the body, but beyond lay the 'inner realisation' of all that one was. When this was recognised, then all needs of the self would be overcome. He said he would be back at the end of the day, and then he quickly turned and left. I felt so alone, and the cold, the darkness and my hunger became my companions.

As the darkness of the room enveloped me, I realised that all I had to do was make my way towards the door and walk free. Free to go home again where warmth and the security of love lay waiting. This thought became my strength, for freedom was only a few steps away. As I contemplated this realisation, a voice within me dared me to walk free.

It spoke to me of my need to experience life with the freedom I had become accustomed to. It reminded me of my family, my friends and the happiness that I felt when I looked out into the night sky and wondered what lay beyond it. I do not know how long my voice spoke to me, but just as I was beginning to realise that my needs were greater than my desire to stay, another voice spoke.

My thoughts suddenly ceased, as I became aware of the power and love that it gave out. It spoke of the quietness of reflection, the detachment of needs and the joy of being part of everything.As I really listened, it became even stronger as it told me of belonging to all and yet belonging to no-one.

I became aware of my body becoming warm, my hunger subsiding and my desire to leave diminishing. As I listened to this voice, I knew that it was a part of me, but the part of me I had not heard before.

Realisation dawned that my voice of desire and need had been my constant companion, and I had not realised there was another part of me that spoke of love in a way I had never thought of before. Tears welled up in my eyes, and my body was racked with emotion that came with this powerful realisation, and I cried for all life everywhere that did not know the love within.

Through the depth of my emotion and discovery, I now became aware that the room had become light. As I looked up, I was startled to see, standing before me, was the Great One.

He smiled, then softly said, "You have done well, you have awakened to the voice within. You will now be taken to be bathed and a new robe will be given to you. Your work now begins."

With those words spoken, He was gone. Almost as if all was known, the door opened and one of the Holy Ones stood within the doorway and asked for me to dress and follow him. As I stood up, I was filled with the wonder of my discovery.

I knew I had found a greater part of who I was. A part that helped me to understand my innermost self. As I placed the robe on, I whispered a silent thank you.

Time passed within the Temple, and the playfulness of youth disappeared. The line between youth and manhood faded as I adjusted more and more to the rigorous program that was set before me. I became acutely aware that I was letting go of 'who' I used to be.

The need I had earlier felt of wanting to be accepted by all within the Temple was over-ridden as I settled into the discipline and teachings of the Brothers. Time was of no consequence, for now I understood that time was only the invention by those who were uncertain of their tomorrows. The vigil of prayer allowed me to identify with my own personal output of love to all within the Temple, as The Brothers spent their days instructing us on the countless ways of loving service towards each other and to all life everywhere.

My first days within the Temple and the memory of meeting the Great One instilled within me an unending desire to be within His presence, but many seasons past by before I was alone with Him once more.

Entering back into the memory of that time, the recollection still enfolds me with that familiar feeling of being aware of the totality of all encompassing love ...

The silence in the courtyard was disturbed by my footsteps as I made my way to the Room of Prayer. The Sun had long set and the Moon had made its way to shining its light upon the far reaches of the courtyard. My thoughts were momentarily stilled, as I sensed a presence that I could not see, yet I was transported into a familiar and powerful awareness of all knowing. I stopped and listened.

My heart raced with anticipation as a figure stepped from the shadows and made its way slowly towards me. It was The Great One. He stood there looking at me with a knowing smile of recognition. My knees felt weak within His presence, and as I allowed the thought of kneeling in front of Him to make itself known, He put his hand up to gesture that I was to stand and that homage was not to be paid to Him.

Then that soft voice that I remembered so well spoke to me. "You have completed the first phase of your life within this Temple and I wish you to collect only a few possessions that can be carried upon your back, and you must leave this Temple for one year and one day. Then you may return, for you will be ready to begin to know."

I stood before Him and my tears of unsureness became mixed up with my great love for Him and for the Temple that I had grown to need so much. Leave here! Where would I go? So many thoughts raced through my mind.

He took a step towards me and placed His hand upon my shoulder. As my eyes looked upwards into His, I surrendered to the understanding that He knew best for me, and that He would always be with me, no matter where my travels took me. I was ready.

The morning light cast shadows upon the dusty pathway, as I trudged slowly along with my few possessions gathered tightly within the small woven cloth that I carried over my shoulder. Where would I go? What would happen to me? Each thought thundered through my mind, and fear was my companion.

I cast my mind back to when He first spoke to me of having the experience of life beyond the Gates of the Temple. "One year and one day", He said. "Have your experience, then come back and tell me what you have learnt". His words echoed within my very being, as I remembered the power of His love.

I now understood that the Gates into the Temple were not the entry into all knowing. For that was an illusion. Knowing was not within the Temple, but in the relationship to all life everywhere.

I visualised those Gates as being non-existent. They were mankind's interpretation of boundaries, and I knew that boundaries did not exist. This realisation showed me not 'who' I was but 'what' I was. If I did not give myself an identity, then I did not exist. Instead I could be found in the oneness where all love existed. This understanding showed me that to put form onto all things prevented one from knowing. The fact was I had not left the Temple, for the Temple was within me.

This revelation empowered me to quicken my step, and I felt an immense feeling of relief that I could be totally at one with all that lay ahead.

The valley lay below shrouded in early morning mist. Smoke from morning fires added to the haze that lay around every-thing. I gazed momentarily at the scene that lay before me, and I allowed myself to reflect on what may have been if I had never entered the Temple.

The young boy who left this valley so long ago - what became of him? As this thought entered my mind, I knew that somewhere within me that young boy still existed, almost as a small voice, but the power of that small voice shocked me with its intensity. As I looked at the valley below, memories came flooding back. Memories I thought I had banished from my mind. I fought back tears as I finally allowed myself to re-member. I remembered my Mother's touch and the tenderness of her voice. I remembered my Father's hands, so big and yet so gentle as he carried me upon his shoulders.

My memories were full of the joy of the times that we shared. The dark nights that were so cold, when we sat around the fire and shared our inner-most thoughts. I also remembered the bad times, when food was scarce, when the rains did not come. All of these memories raced around and around my mind.

Slowly I made my way down the mountainside. The village was still the same, with so many reminders of the past. The old tree that had stood forever, challenging all to climb to the top. How I had longed to have had the courage to climb it, as the older boys had. The top of that tree always seemed somehow so far out of reach.

The large rock that seemed to stand guard at the entrance to the village. The engraving upon it bore witness to many a young person that had long since taken leave. All was so familiar. I walked on, reminding myself that I was only on leave and there was no permanency to this endeavour. Time stood still. All revealed its memory to me, and yet my heart ached for another place, a place of absolute peace and stillness.

The Temple. The Temple had been my home for so long, but the memory of this village seemed to take delight in challenging all memories of my time within the silence and tranquillity of the Temple. However, I found I was able to allow all thoughts and memory to take their rightful place without any conflict.

It would have been so easy to have become a victim of memory, and yet within the memory of the times of my childhood spent within this village, an emptiness grew, as I felt the most powerful memory of all, the memory of the Temple within.

For all memories of my early childhood stood only as a shadow within the light of the love that I had uncovered within the Temple. Within my heart I realised that whatever memory I had, it held no connection to what I had become. Belonging was not to a place, but was within the knowing that there was never a time that we did not belong. That was the illusion.

My entry into the village was quickly noticed, for a member of the Priesthood to enter into the village was rare indeed. My simple white robe and shaven heard aroused the curiosity of the children who ran to my side in anticipation that I was carrying gifts from the Temple for the people of the village.

When I assured them that all I had upon me was a few simple possessions, they soon lost interest and I was once again able to continue my journey. I quickened my pace and entered into the heart of the village that was so familiar to me. My heart raced with anticipation at my family's reaction to my homecoming, and I smiled inwardly as I knocked at the door of the place that I once called home.

The door slowly opened, and there before me was the loving face of my dear Mother. Her eyes widened with amazement as she registered recognition of who I was. Her tears were my tears as she threw her arms around me and held me tightly to her. This was the moment that I had never allowed myself to think of.

This was the moment that I had feared. The fear of separation of love. As I held on tightly to that love, I knew that what I felt within my Mother's love was not separate from the love that I knew within the Temple. They were one and the same.

I realised then that I did not need to feel fear within love for it held no comparison for me, and within that knowing there was freedom. I had not allowed myself to acknowledge the memory of my Mother's love within the Temple, lest I felt a need to find a comparison to the love of all.

As the Great One had said, "Love was all the same. From the inner to the outer, it knew no comparison." How right He was, but I had to discover that by myself, and this I had done.

The day that followed was a day that I will always hold within my heart. Our laughter and joy must have sounded out throughout the entire village, for so many came and enquired about my welfare.

Within a village, nothing can be kept quiet for long, and the news of my arrival was known by all as the Sun finally set.

As the Sun disappeared from view and my eyes closed to the day that had just passed, I sent quiet thanks to the Great One for this day. Sleep engulfed me and I surrendered to it.

The morning light came swiftly. I stirred as the first rays of light entered, for the discipline of early rising was strongly embedded within me. I quickly dressed and stepped outside.

One day had passed. I had one more year before I was able to enter the Temple once again. The one year could not be spent in the village, this I knew. For to do so would be foolish, for nothing could be learnt, for nothing would be new.

As I gazed upon the splendour of the Mountains that lay all around, my thoughts drifted back to the Temple. Was it only one day that had passed since I had left the sanctuary of its peace?

My heart felt heavy at the need to leave behind the safety and love that lay within its walls.

How different I had become. How little I realised this until I was confronted with the past. The young boy who feared to leave the security of his home and his family. Where had he gone? As these thoughts entered my mind, I was startled by a voice that demanded my attention.

"Can you help an old man?" I looked around to see a very old man clothed like a beggar. It was obvious that his sight was failing as he had in his left hand a small staff, which he used to help him recognise any obstacles in front of him, and he was heading my way.

"I need help to cross the Mountains," he said. "I have just received news that a friend needs me. I need your help. We will leave soon, so go and get what is necessary for the trip."

"Just a moment," I said. "I would like to help you, but I cannot. I have things to attend to and family to share time with. You will have to find someone else. I would surely like to help you, but it is not possible."

"I will not take no for an answer," he said. "I need to start my journey as soon as possible, and you will do very nicely as my guide. My eyes do not work as well as they used to, but your eyes are young and they will show me the way."

My mind went back to my earlier thoughts, that to stay within the village for too long would be foolish, and yet I did not feel ready to leave. For only one day had passed and there was still one year before me.

So I replied, "No, old man, I am sorry but I cannot go with you for I am not ready to leave, not quite yet."

His voice was quiet, but stern as he took one more step towards me. "Young man, I am not asking you, but I am telling you. You are to take me across the Mountains this day. When the Sun is high within the sky, you will meet me here with food and water to last us several days."

With those words spoken, he turned and walked away. His appearance gave little indication of the authority in his voice, and as I struggled to call out and voice my opposition to his words, somehow I knew that it would be useless to do so.

Instead I resigned myself to accept his need as being greater than mine. I consoled myself with the thought that perhaps a journey beyond the Mountains would allow me to be of service to one who is handicapped through age and sight.

Yes, I thought, to be in service to another who is less fortunate would be a great opportunity to share the love and care I hold within. The Great One would be well pleased with me!

The Sun was high in the sky as I made my way to meet the old man. True to his word, he was there waiting for me, and as I approached he lifted his head so as to indicate that he had indeed recognised my footsteps upon the rocky ground.

Questions kept returning to my mind as I relived the moment that this old man came into my life. Why did he insist upon me taking him across the Mountains? I had not lived within the village for many years, and in fact was unsure as to the best path to take.

For one who looked so frail, he commanded an air of power. However, something puzzled me. No-one in the village knew of the old man. I had questioned many, but to no avail. Not even one person could remember such an old man living anywhere near the village.

However, the new-found desire to be of service to one who was nearly without sight, plus my inbuilt need for adventure, prompted me to meet the old man, as he asked. A few days was surely little sacrifice when I had one year left to uncover the wisdom of life away from the Temple walls.

As I drew closer to him, I noticed that his feet were bare of any covering and he did not have in his possession any warm blanket for the cold nights to come. He was ill prepared for the long walk across the Mountains.

How strange he was, and yet he had a presence about him that stopped me from further questioning him. If he chose to not bring warm clothing and a blanket upon the journey, then so be it. That was his choice. I felt reassured as I gently patted my pack upon my back, knowing that I was well prepared, even if he was not.

He turned, and without speaking at all, started to walk towards the path leading to the Mountain track that lay in the distance.

He certainly was not one for words, but yet the solitude would be familiar to me, as the training within the Temple had given me the ability to not use the voice of the body, when one is using the voice of the "Inner".

For one who has little sight, he was quite confident upon the even ground. No doubt he would need my help when the journey took on a more treacherous pathway. It felt good to have the Sun and the wind upon me, and I even began to look forward to the journey ahead.

We walked through the day and into the early evening without one word being exchanged. The old man seemed more intent in keeping his thoughts to himself, as we journeyed up the Mountain track.

As the Sun started to set, I became a little weary and my hunger and thirst prompted me to remind the old man that we needed to stop and rest for the night. As the night cast its shadow, the image of the journey started to take on a feeling of unsureness. The night air became chilled as the Sun no longer warmed the place upon where I sat.

The old man looked upwards towards the sky, almost as if, in his blindness, he was seeing something that I could not. The night played its part well, as the shadows grew longer and the sounds of the day changed over to the sounds of the night.

As I looked at the old man, I wondered, "Who was he? Why did he need to cross the Mountain with someone like myself, who did not have any experience of this journey at all? Not like others of the village who had travelled this way many times before."

He turned his head and I clearly felt his gaze on me. How ridiculous I thought. He is nearly blind, he cannot see me. Yet I felt very uneasy.

"The body needs food and water," he said. "Make haste and build a fire so a meal can be prepared and the body warmed. For the body needs to be recognised and rewarded for the journey it has made today."

For just a moment the imprint of his words struck inwardly, as if a familiar sound was registered. I quickly shrugged this thought off, for surely the mind was playing tricks. He was only an old blind man. I had spent time with him before this day.

I quickly went about the business of preparing the food and allowed the small flame of the fire to grow in strength. A simple meal was cooked and quickly eaten. This was done in silence, except for the sounds of small animals within the shadows, eyeing us carefully in case there was evidence of any food left over from the meal.

I felt so tired from the day's travelling, that sleep quickly overtook me. As I closed my eyes, all I remember is the old man sitting and gazing into the flame of the fire. Within my sleep, visions of the past showed themselves. I was once again within the Temple, seated and listening to the Great One who was speaking to all who had gathered.

"The power of love is unknown," He said. "The power of life does not allow the power of love to be known. The inner destiny of your life is to know this fact. For without the imprint of your life, you would never have known the illusion of love.

You are all emissaries of illusion. Be aware of that. If you believe that you are emissaries of light, then you have taken the wrong turn upon your pathway. For the joy of illusion is to embrace it with all that you are, so that through the acknowledgment of that what it is, you can finally let it go.

When you look for love, all you will find is illusion. The pathway through illusion will lead you to love."

The Great One's words rang within my sleep, and the joy of listening to His words was still with me when I awoke. The Sun had not as yet risen as I stirred into awakening. The old man lay still sleeping as I made way to the stream to bathe my body from the dust of the day before. The water was cold, but yet it revived my body into action.

My mind went back to the memories within the night, and my heart leapt with the joy of remembering. How easy it was to forget and to become caught up with what lay outside the walls of the Temple. I drew strength from my memories, and reproached myself for not allowing my daytime thoughts to have connected also to what the Great One had said.

As the water embraced my body, I allowed my thoughts to encompass the coming day. To be in service to an old blind man, surely that was the most important aspect of the day.

However, I had to make sure that my thoughts did not keep returning to my reluctance in leaving my family for the journey that I had undertaken with the old man.

I dressed quickly, and made my way back, so that I could prepare the morning meal. The old man was still seated next to the fire.

He turned towards me and said, "I have decided that we will stay here. We will not be venturing any further upon this day."

I started to choke on my words. "Why?" I asked. "Surely you need to continue on your journey so you can be with your friend who needs you!"

"My need is greater to stay here," he replied. "That is all I have to say." With those words, he gazed back into the flame of the fire.

That was one more day I had lost in my venture to experience life away from the Temple. My time away from the Temple was surely testing me.

The day moved on so very slowly as I contemplated how to approach the old man with my need to make haste, so that I could complete my journey with him. I wanted so much to return back to the village.

Chapter 3

The old man seemed mesmerised with the flame of the fire, and his gaze never faltered for a moment. In that moment I decided there was nothing else to do but to join him, and so I took my place opposite him and reluctantly looked into the flame of the fire.

As the flame flickered and danced, my inner vision seemed to play tricks on me. For a moment the old man appeared to transform into the vision of the Great One. Much to my surprise and astonishment, the vision then spoke to me and said, "Come with me into the flame of knowing, and take the journey of remembrance upon this day."

The flame of the fire disappeared and I was once again within the Temple walls. There was darkness all around me, except for the light of the Moon that hovered above. The silence enveloped me as I found myself within the Inner part of the Temple, where none is allowed to enter, unless they have passed the test of 'remembrance'.

What was I doing here? I wondered. For I knew no-one was permitted to be within this part of the Temple, unless they had passed the final test of remembrance. I had not.

I felt a sense of confusion and panic, as I began to search for a way in which to leave. It was then that I suddenly came face to face with the Great One.

My words of apology tumbled over each other as I tried to explain my confusion of being within this part of the Temple, which had always barred me from entering.

"I do not know how I came to be here, but I will now leave," I said. His gentle voice echoed through the room. "You will not leave, for it was I who brought you here. You are now within the Inner Temple of Remembrance because I need to show you something. You will be seated."

With those words spoken, He gestured to me to join him upon the stone floor, as He took his place upon one of the woven mats.

"Where are you?" He asked. "Are you within the Inner Temple of Remembrance, or are you outside the walls of the Temple experiencing the illusion of a journey across the Mountains? Where is your reality upon this day?" As I listened to what He said, I became totally confused within my mind.

My memory went back to the old man seated around the fire, looking into the flickering flame. I also had taken my place around the fire, so as to still my frustration that the journey was taking far too long across the Mountains. That was my last memory.

What was I doing here? How did I get here? Was all this a dream?

"Whose dream is this? Is it my dream or yours?" As He spoke those words, I looked up into his eyes, that seemed to find amusement at my confusion, and yet, within his amusement I felt the seriousness of his words.

How could I answer that question? My thoughts raced around and around my mind.

He looked at me and said, "I all depends upon who has the power within the dream. That is your answer."

"What do you mean when you say power?" I asked. "If it was my dream, then can I change the dream whenever I wish?"

"Yes," He replied. "That is your right."

The power of his words took a moment to find their mark. If this was my dream, then I could create or change anything within it! As my excitement at this prospect started to mount, his next words quickly changed everything.

"However, if this is my dream, then I have the power and not yourself. If this is the case, the dream is in my hands alone!"

He rose to his feet and gestured that I also do the same. As I stood up I held my breath, wondering what would be revealed next. I didn't have long to wait.

"Tell me, whose dream is this?" He asked. I replied, "I believe it is mine. For I am upon a Mountain with an old man who is nearly blind. I am his guide across the Mountain, so that he can be with another who is ailing. If I am upon the Mountain, I surely cannot be here within the Temple. Yes, that is my answer. It is surely my dream."

He looked at me and smiled. "Then show me the power that you have. Change your dream! I am waiting."

I felt the challenge within His words, and yet I felt hesitant as to what to do next.

"What are you waiting for?" He asked. "Are you fearful for what is to be revealed? That it is I who has the power and not yourself."

"I do not know how to change my dream," I replied. "I know that I am asleep upon the Mountain, but I do not know how to get back there."

"You are very sure that this is your dream," He said. "All I ask is for you to prove it."

He continued, "Why do you not wake up and cease this dream? If it is your dream as you say, then surely you have the power to do that, but if it is my dream, then surely it is my choice as to when you awaken. That is then my right, and I have the power to awaken you."

I felt his words echo through my very being. Even through the depth of my confusion I became aware of a peace, like no other I had ever experienced.

Why did I need the power within the dream? If I let go of the power, then surely the dream would reveal itself.

He looked at me and smiled. "I believe you know whose dream this is."

"Yes," I replied. "It is your Dream. I now know that to be true." As I spoke those words, the room completely changed before my eyes. I felt the floor beneath me falling away, and the walls that seemed so solid a moment ago, just seemed to vanish in an instant.

I felt His hands upon my shoulders, and I was enveloped in a blurred sensation of spinning around and around. Within this sensation, came a feeling of great warmth and a sense of being absolutely sheltered from all fear and unsureness.

As I surrendered completely to all that was happening to me, I became aware for the very first time of not wanting to control my destiny. I now knew that destiny was the illusion of life, and within our life we create our destiny.

These thoughts came to an abrupt halt as the spinning stopped, and I heard His voice once again. "Open your eyes and tell me what you see".

I slowly opened my eyes and found myself within a City that appeared bathed in light. At first it seemed the light was Silver, but as I looked more closely, the light actually shimmered with so many colours they blended together harmoniously, as if to make the light dance.

"Where are we?" I asked. "Are we within the Heaven of the Gods?"

He laughed and replied, "No, we are not within the City of Image and Illusion, but instead we are within the City of Remembrance. This is the place where all come who finally remember the illusion of their life."

My mind raced with so many thoughts and questions, but yet I felt incapable of saying anything at all. Instead I stood transfixed with wonder and absolute joy at the sight before me.

I took a deep breath to regain some sort of composure and asked, "Why have you brought me here, when I do not remember? Yet I know I am within the confines of illusion within my thoughts, that too often over-run my sense of remembering."

"You so quickly forget," He said. "You so quickly forget it is my dream and I have the power to help you remember. I want you to follow me, for we are to go to the Inner Chamber of Remembrance that awaits us, even as I speak."

He beckoned me to follow Him, and we made our way slowly into the City itself. I must be dreaming I thought. And with this thought I laughed to myself. Oh, the illusion of it all. I have already forgotten this is not my dream after all.

I laughed out loud at this understanding, and I felt so comfortable and so free, as I looked forward to what lay ahead. Whatever it was, I knew I had no control over it. What a relief!

As we entered into the heart of the City I was overcome by the feeling I had been here before. It was just so familiar and yet I had to question how that could be, for I had no memory of ever being within this place before. However, a strange feeling engulfed me, and I bit hard upon my lip to stop the emotion from overflowing. My body felt wracked with the need to express the feelings I felt, as I started to remember that I had, in fact, been here before. In fact, I now knew I had been here many times before.

I felt myself question the feelings I was experiencing, yet I knew that no matter what thoughts I uttered within my mind, nothing could take away my response that everything was, oh so familiar.

The Great One stopped, almost as if He knew what was happening with my struggle to understand what I was experiencing. He looked at me in the way He always did when He was about to reveal something I needed to know.

"You are within the City of Remembrance," He said. "Yet you struggle so hard to discount what you are feeling and what you are remembering, because you are so pre-occupied with needing to substantiate whether, in fact, you have been here before."

"Yes, that is so," I replied. "My memory says I have not been here before, yet it is all so familiar. Why is that?"

He placed his hand upon my shoulder and said, "Whilst you are within memory, illusionary memory, you are not able to remember. When your memory ceases to be your reference point of knowing, you will remember all. When you try so hard to remember, all you are experiencing is the illusion within memory that time and space dictates.

I have brought you here so that you can release your illusion of memory that has been your guiding influence within your life. The power you have given up unto that memory has allowed you to view even what I am through an image that you have created.

When you speak of remembering, I wonder what it is that you remember? Is it that you remember you have been here before, or are you remembering that you do not remember what you know to be a fact?"

I listened to his words and I wondered as to whether I really understood what memory really was. I thought that memory could be explained by re-living a past experience within action, or learning by bringing it forward within the mind to re-examine it, and use it as a reference point to another thought or another action.

Now I was not so sure. For He was telling me that memory was illusion, and if that was so, what did my life mean?

"Come," He said. "We must not linger. For they await."

"Who are waiting?" I asked.

"You will soon see, He replied.

As we walked through the City streets, my vision took in as much as it could to equal the pace that we were travelling. Whilst the City from afar gave a silvery hue, the buildings up close took on a variation of colours. Colours that seemed to emit a sound that changed from building to building.

I felt a desire to reach out and touch the walls as we quickly passed by, but as soon as this thought was registered, I realised that to do so would be foolish, for it would certainly hinder the pace of our journey.

On the way back, I decided, there would be time to explore, for surely I have not been brought to this place to stay for only a short while.

The feeling of familiarity had gone. Almost as if it was a thought that was not of my making. Where were the people I wondered? Are we alone within this place? Perhaps those who live in this City are inside the buildings. Yes, that must be right. For who had heard of a City where there were no people.

Our journey came to an abrupt halt as we stood before a doorway to a simple white building that was somehow a little different from those we had passed. There was no variation of colour, just a white glow that seemed to awaken a feeling of uncertainty within me.

I felt a reluctance to enter that I could not quite understand. My throat started to tighten and my stomach turned over and over. What was it about this place that caused my very being to question my relationship to all that was within me?

The Great One turned and said, "Be not afraid, for all that you are is to be understood. Take my hand, and we shall venture within together."

As I took his hand I felt the power of His love overcome the illusion of my fear. The door opened and we made our way into a very large room that was completely empty.

"We will wait here,"He said. "We will await their presence."

As I stood within that room I felt like a small child. Who were they, and what did they want from me? I didn't have long to wait, for I was suddenly confronted with an amazing sight.

Within the centre of the room a shaft of light appeared, and from that light a figure stepped out, dressed in a golden robe. His hair was also golden, and within his hand he held a staff.

The Great One stepped forward to greet him, and I stood absolutely still, so as to not create a ripple within the image that I was seeing.

"I have brought the boy as you requested," He said.

"That is good," said the Golden One. "The others will be here in a moment, they will not be long".

And with a sweep of his hand, the room was suddenly transformed, so as to include many seats that seemed to be made of marble. "Please be seated for there is much to discuss and much to uncover."

I did as He asked, but felt that I needed to enquire of Him, what in fact was needed to be discussed, or even uncover? Was I brave enough to even allow myself to speak, lest my tongue becomes paralysed mid-sentence? I decided against it, for surely to wait was the better way.

My mind became still as I ceased the endless thoughts that so often trapped me into an evaluation of my surroundings. And within the stillness of my mind came a surge of anticipation and excitement for what was to take place.

I sat transfixed, looking towards the centre of the room and waited. I didn't have long to wait, for another shaft of light entered the centre of the room, as before. I sat forward straining to see, not wanting to miss anything.

7 figures stepped out of the light into the room. Each one was dressed in a simple white robe, and tied around their waist was a golden sash. Their feet were bare and they held in their hands a glowing ball of light.

As they emerged, they were greeted by the Golden One. He embraced each one in a Brotherly way, as they made their way towards the seats. When they were all seated, the Golden One stood and addressed me.

"We have come so you may understand the value of life. We believe you have misunderstood that what you seek. All is hidden from view when the vision comes from your mind. All cannot be heard when the sound does not find its mark upon the centre of your Being. And yet, all that you see and hear is through the illusion of your thoughts.

You are within the dream of the future, and yet some call it the past. You have been re-created so that the future can be recalled into the past. Your image of your now is centred through your illusionary memory to your past. However, we now allow you to view that what is rightfully yours.

Within the fabric of creation comes a story yet to unfold. It involves the journey through a vast array of images that criss-cross into a range of patterns. Each pattern is in opposing ends to another, and so on, until all patterns are experienced into the vastness of that which was first recognised. All is within a rotunda of evolutions. Each one offering up a program of rela-tivity that records each round of possibilities. You are indeed one of those possibilities that have been sent into the fabric of illusion.

You have recorded your beginnings within the imagery of time, and yet you are more than that. You are within the image of this dream, so that the storyteller can experience that what you are. Perhaps it was you that expected to experience that what the storyteller could not."

His words raced through my mind, and I wondered if He really expected me to understand what He was saying.

I obviously had a look of confusion upon my face, for He continued. "You have been brought here before us so you can measure your illusion. Within the measurement of illusion comes a need to evaluate what is no longer required, to be carried into the tomorrow. You are within a dream, but not of your making.

You are the participant that allows the dream to unfold, yet you are wondering why you need to understand illusion at all, if you did not create it in the first place."

As I listened to those words, I was in agreement with Him. For why was I brought here to look at what was not real, if in fact the dream was not mine?

He smiled at me, as if He knew my thoughts. "What if illusion did not exist at all, but the thought that it was illusion was the reason for its existence?"

That really confused me. How could illusion know illusion? That didn't make any sense at all.

"What is your life? What power do you have within it?" He asked. "Answer me."

I gulped at the need to speak up, and my hesitation was not lost to Him.

He continued. "You are indeed not aware of the power that you have within your life whilst you do not acknowledge the power of illusion. You always look for the power within the fullness of what you are, within the higher imprint of light that creates all. Whilst you deny that illusion has power, you indeed deny the power you have within illusion.

You have directed your need rather than the storyteller's need to uncover illusion. I ask you this - within the dream, not of your making, what purpose is your life if, in fact, you believe that your life is only the illusion of another?"

I nodded my head in agreement, for what was the purpose of it all if I was a character in someone's dream? I would just wait for the dream to finish surely, if I, the character, was aware that it was only a dream and it was not under my control.

"That is where you have gone wrong so far," He said. Obviously knowing my thoughts as He had done before.

"Where is the core of the dream? Why was the dream started in the first instance? For what purpose is the dream of life? If you are to understand illusion, then you have to understand why illusion was created in the first place."

My whole being responded to His words, almost as if I had heard them once before, somewhere. He looked at me, waiting for me to reply.

Illusion. Is every thought camouflaged with illusion and yet calls itself reality? How can thought belong to another and yet I adopt it as my own, and act out the part of its illusion? How can I truly answer when all I have is my own thoughts of what illusion may or may not be?

From where would I base my answer? Would it be from my memories of all my actions that came from my thought, or would I offer it up as if I was completely oblivious to the power of what illusion may or may not be to me? He was obviously waiting for my answer, and yet I did not have one to give Him.

He recognised immediately my unsureness as to how, in fact, I was going to answer Him. His eyes seemed to search into my very being, almost as if He expected me to try and find a suitable answer that would assure Him that I understood completely the message within His words.

The best thing to do, I decided, was to just shrug my shoulders and shake my head and say absolutely nothing! And that is what I did. I wondered how long I would have to wait before He either turned away from me in complete disgust at my lack of comprehension, or He would insist upon an answer immediately.

I held my breath and waited, but silence has a way of making unsureness even more acute. He said nothing. Absolutely nothing! He just kept looking at me, as if, by some chance, I would suddenly jump up with delight and tell Him, "Yes, I have the answer!"

My mind was on overload, with so many thoughts racing round and round, trying to overcome my embarrassment, hoping to come up with some great statement or vision that would allow Him to see that I was indeed blessed with a great awareness and inner awakening.

"Give me your hand," He said. Isn't it amazing, even at that point, I had to make a decision as to which hand I would give Him.

The tension was completely broken as He laughed out loud. "Action should be automatic, not a decision that allows thought to analyse why an action should or should not be.

You cannot even make up your mind about which hand you should give me because you have a choice. However, if I had told you which hand to give me, then I would have made the choice for you, and you would not have had indecision.

Your life has been created so that thought can uncover the need to acknowledge the power behind the thought. Within each ones life comes a need to appraise the value of thought and to identify why thought has created the value of ones life.

When we speak of illusion, we are speaking of a thought. If you believe in the value of that thought, you would call it reality. However, when you see the true nature of thought, then you would see the illusion within it.

Thought instigates action, would you agree?"

"Yes," I said, "of course. For without thought no action would be taken".

"Who is responsible for thought" He asked.

"Surely the person who created the thought," I replied.

He looked at me and shook his head and said, "When you identify a thought as being the very first thought ever uttered, then you may give that answer. However, all thought has been created before. You are unable to create a new thought, for all you are doing is drawing upon thought and placing your need for re-creating it and then placing action within it, and then you call it your own."

He continued, "Whilst thought is divisible, it is not an original thought. The power within thought allows for creation to exist. Evolution within creation is decided upon by the power of thought that allows it to exist.

Evolution is the core of the dream. Evolving through thought, so that thought can finally be stilled. For when thought is acknowledged, it is no longer needed, for it has found its mark in its incompleteness.

You are an incomplete thought that allows for illusion to exist. You are the participant within the dream. And you would ask who or what in fact is the power behind the dream."

"Yes, you are right," I said. "For if everything is incomplete because of thought, then why does the dream continue? And who or what is the power behind it all?"

"You would have to firstly understand the power of illusion within thought before you could even start to understand the power behind it," He replied.

"Close your eyes," He said. "and don't open them until I tell you to do so."

I did as He instructed. A few moments went past until He said, "Now open them and tell me what you see."

As I looked around me I was completely shocked to find that the room had disappeared. The room had gone! We were standing within 'nothing'. There were no visible points of reference, only light.

"Where did the room go?:" I asked, somewhat feebly.

"You are seeing your surroundings without any thought being attached to them. Your surroundings are still there, except that I have removed the thought of their existence. Without thought, all things cannot exist."

"I am still here and you are still here," I said. "Surely we are also a result of thought, and if that is the case, then why are we still here?" I was pleased with my line of questioning, for surely He would now see I had something to contribute.

"You are surely right," He said. "All is created by thought. However, within the power of thought comes a need to understand the result of thought, as against its need to create itself. For within the power of the 'All that is' is an endowment of light. That light is the power source that allows thought to be incomplete.

Many believe that thought is the way to the understanding of the inner realisation of what one calls truth. However, the energy source of 'true and complete thought' is ever-present within all that is not complete.

If you can understand the power of incompleteness within thought, then you must understand the completeness within it also. They are within two opposing ends, allowing each one to exist so that the boundary between the need to create and the need to not create can be substantiated.

Your life has been, so far, a duplicate of needing to create and not create. Surely you can see that."

I listened carefully to what He was saying. Yes, I thought to myself, I understood that the Temple allowed me to view life differently, so that incompleteness turned into itself and allowed completeness to follow. But when any doubts entered into my mind, then all that was left was my need to find a reason for why I needed to place a thought into action.

He allowed my thoughts to finish, before He continued, "All are upon a journey of Inward Reflection, and because of this fact, there needs to be an adjudicator behind all thought in case thought tries to take all control from the Dreamer."

"Tell me more about the dream," I said. "I really do not understand how my life is connected to someone else's dream. Could you please tell me more, so I can understand it better?"

"Yes, I will answer you," He replied. "However, we firstly need to allow our surroundings to return."

Just as these words were spoken, I found myself back in the room. The other Beings were also there, still seated across from me, as they were before. The Golden One smiled as He obviously viewed my amazement at how quickly all could return back to the way it was before.

He beckoned for the Great One to join us, which He did. And so we sat, the three of us together, as I received the message and the meaning of what the dream really meant.

"What is the difference between the dreamer and the dream?" the Golden One asked me. "As you look at the dream, can you, in fact, recognise the dreamer within it?

If you regard the dreamer and the dream as different from each other, then what comparison is made so that the difference is identified? The dream is always identified by the dreamer as being a creation that does not confound the actuality of recognising that there is, indeed, a difference between the dreamer and the dream.

Whilst the dreamer has the power to instil the formula for what is to take place, the dream is the resultant image of that."

I listened carefully to what He had to say. However, I knew I was somehow missing the main ingredient. Why was the dream created in the first place? What power, if any, did the character in the dream have?

He looked at me and smiled, and turning to the Great One he said, "The young man is coming to terms that the power is not necessarily in his hands. His mind betrays his confusion that does not belong to the dreamer."

The Great One nodded in agreement but said nothing. The Golden One continued. "Are you the result of the dream, or are you within a formation of possibilities that allows you to fulfil one of those possibilities within the character that you are?

If you agree that you are the result of the dream, then that would not allow you the free will that you believe you have in your life.

All would be pre-ordained, and therefore you would only re-enact one possibility that allows for the dream to unfold".

My mind raced back to what He had told me earlier when He spoke of myself being one possibility within a dream, and if that was the case, then could there be more than one possibility through someone else within the same dream? Or was it up to me to create more possibilities so that other characters could be brought into the dream?

Something stirred within me, as if I was so close to erasing something that had been with me all of my life. That barrier which always seemed to stand between what I believed I represented and what lay beyond that.

The Golden One suddenly stood up and addressed the 7 Beings that were seated. "Stand my Brothers and come and be with us." ◊Each one stood and approached Him, still holding onto the balls of light they held in their hands.

"Show the young man what you have within your hands," He said. "Show him the power of light that each one has within their grasp."

As His words rang through the room, I felt touched by the power within them, and yet they were soft and gentle.

I watched as each of the 7 Beings joined together within a circle and held their hands up towards the centre. Each ball of light within their hands started to glow and pulsate.

The balls of light started to change colour, and in rapid succession each ball changed from one colour to another, to another. My eyes could not keep up with the rapid changes, and my head was spinning and I felt breathless.

Something was happening to me that I did not understand. All I knew was the power I felt within my inner being could not be explained in words. There were no words to describe what was happening. I felt completeness like I had never felt before.

Somewhere in the back of my mind I heard the Golden One speak to me. "Keep watching, for soon you will see the power that each one has within their hands if they choose to use it." I did as He told me and my eyes strained to see it all and not miss anything.

The Golden One spoke again. "The power of the 7 will now reveal the power of one." The room started to go dark, except for the illumination of the balls of light that were being held up towards the centre of the circle.

Each ball suddenly became bigger and bigger until each one touched the edge of the other, and before my very eyes, the 7 balls became one.

The Golden One then said, "Within the power of the 7 Universes comes only one light. There is no separation between one acknowledgement and another, except through the power of thought. That thought comes from beyond the power of 7, so that the separation of energy that you know as the self identity is seen as only a very small part of the separation value of all life."

"7 Universes!" I said. "There are 7 Universes?" I could not keep back my surprise.

"No," He said. "That is the point. There is only one Universe operating through 7 possibilities. Each one is a definition of a dream.

So 7 dreams have been created with the same outcome intact. The dreamer and the dream are one and the same. However, the dreamer has decided that the character in the dream will take on the part of not remembering, so that evolution of illusion can be maintained."

I heard His words as if I had heard them before. They were familiar and yet they were not. As I started to question what this meant, somehow I lost the feeling of completeness that I had felt just a moment before. I became confused, totally and utterly confused.

Where was all this leading to, and why had I been brought here? What point was there in showing me 7 balls of light going into one, if I was a character within a dream that was not supposed to remember?

Surely that was a contradiction. I turned my attention once again to what was happening within the centre of the room. The light of the one ball was pulsating. I watched it pulsate, and then something happened. I felt the pulsation within my very being.

I don't know how long this went on for, but suddenly I had the greatest urge to approach the light. It was almost as if it was sending out a thought and calling me!

I fought hard to keep seated, and then in desperation I turned to the Golden One and said, "Why is it that I need to go within the light? Why is it that I feel the power of it within my very being? And if I was denied this request, why is it that I know that I would always feel incomplete?"

What was I saying? What was happening to me? The power of that light was like nothing I had ever experienced before. It went even beyond the power that I felt with the Great One when we first met.

It was as if I was that light, and to be away from it would be to deny all that I was. How easy it was to doubt when you are not focused upon that light. How easy it was for me to question the purpose of this moment, when I did not view it through the power of that light. The Golden One addressed me.

"Go, and enter into the light. It is waiting for you."

I did as He said. I stood up and slowly approached the centre of the room. The closer that I came to that light, the more that I knew that the light was waiting for me. I felt no fear. I only felt the need to become one with that light, as if I had been away from it for, oh so long. I made my way through the circle of Beings and entered into the light. A rush of energy surged within me, as I felt the absolute completeness of all.

The room disappeared from view, and yet I knew, as before, that it was still there, but I was beyond the thought that created it. I was beyond all time and space. I knew that I was complete and all that lay beyond was incomplete.

The character I was, beyond the light, was only a thought. Whilst I was within that light, I knew that I had created that thought, and that the power that I am has allowed that thought to be a part of the illusion, that allowed all to recognise that what I was.

Whilst I was within this understanding, and indeed the very knowing that all is complete, I reached within the energy that I was to recall what I had created, as to the life of the character I am.

The early days of my childhood flashed before me. My entry into the Temple. The fear I had created so that I understood the power of the illusion of fear when first I left the security of my family.

The memory of the Great One, when first we met, that allowed me to view the limitedness of my acknowledgment of that what I was. The year and one day that was required to see a different perspective away from the Temple.

The old man upon the Mountain who allowed me to view the illusion of service. To see the incompleteness of what the self was when it was given an opportunity to divert from what it believed it should be doing.

All this I had created, and I knew, I actually knew why I had created it all.

But the most powerful knowing of all was that I now knew that I was dreaming upon that Mountain, and that I had decided to view the dreamer, so that I could understand within the dream the power that I had.

Fear, distrust and illusion were only a part of the character that I had created. I also had the power to change the role of the character if I chose. It all depended upon the value within the illusion. As long as illusion attracted the power of non-illusion to it, then the dream could continue without any new characters being created.

However, once the power within illusion magnified into more illusion, then more characters were needed to over-ride the power within it. More possibilities were created in order to retract the fear back into the illusion of not needing it at all.

The times of the past disappeared as the future unfolded. I saw my character enter the Inner Sanctuary...

It was a dark night, and as my footsteps echoed upon the stone steps, I hurried into the doorway of the Inner Sanctuary.

They had already started and I made my way silently towards the back and sat down upon the cold stone floor. He was speaking. The one they called the 'Father of All'. He was dressed in his gown of Indigo and the radiance was as beautiful as it always was.

I looked momentarily around me, not wanting to take my gaze and attention away from He that knew me so well, but to look lovingly at the Temple that brought me so much joy, so much sorrow, so much pain, and yet here I was, seated with the knowing of my real self, and it was He that I now knew to be the Father of All.

The room was fairly wide, with a long narrow opening to allow the night sky to be visible upon the upper reaches of the room. The night was dark, the moon not yet visible, but the room seemed somehow so very light with the presence of the wondrous beings that knew us so well.

He speaks of belonging. Not to an individual, not to a belief, not to any one thing, but to belong totally within all.

He says that belonging can be looked upon as a dependency of thought that allows another to take advantage, but in the belonging to all there is a knowing that there can never be a separateness of thought, ever.

As He speaks, I turn inwardly to the belonging of all, and I allow a single thought to remind me of my insecurity of letting go of the outward belonging.

A simple thought, but yet as it is uttered from my mind, I open my eyes to see Him looking at me, and I know that He knows that I am not ready yet to enter into the oneness of all.

My inner being screams to be allowed to be given an opportunity to try again, but I can feel the failure welling up within me, which is my fear of letting go of who I believe myself to be, and so with a heavy heart I stand and leave the sanctity of the Inner Chamber.

Failure has no part to play in the uncovering of the Greater Plan, and yet as I look back upon that day of knowing that my inner search has not passed the test of letting go completely, I shall re-enter the Temple of Remembrance once again, and I shall know...

All was so clear within the light of all. I am the dreamer and yet I am the dream. The dream is to be re-run over and over again until the character within the dream recognises that they are, in fact, the dreamer.

Only then will the illusion cease. For thought no longer allows it to continue.

I am the dreamer. I am the light. All else does not exist.

YOU ARE WITHIN THE DREAM OF

YOUR OWN MAKING

YOU ARE THE DREAM MAKER

WHEN YOU WAKE UP AND KNOW THAT

THEN THE DREAM IS OVER

Available Reading:

**The Journey Home
with Elonias**
Diane Swaffield

The Greatest Story Never Told
Amoen, Diane Swaffield

Upon the Sands of Time
Diane Swaffield

A Life Worth Living
Diane Swaffield

Available Viewing:

'The Illusion of Reality' Documentary
Written, produced & Narrated by Jason Swaffield

Online Resources:

eloniasfoundation.com
thetimecentre.com